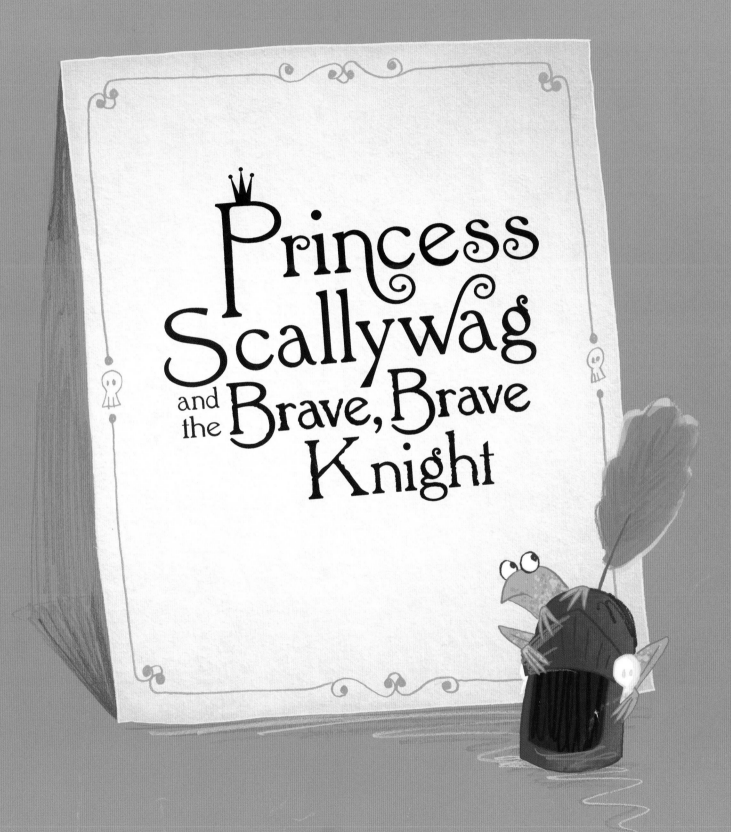

Princess Scallywag and the Brave, Brave Knight

For Jess B
–M. S.

For Simba–ROAAAR!
–C. P.

First published in paperback in Great Britain by HarperCollins Children's Books in 2018
This edition published in 2019

1 3 5 7 9 10 8 6 4 2

ISBN: 978-0-00-832597-8

HarperCollins Children's Books is a division of HarperCollins Publishers Ltd.

Text copyright © Mark Sperring 2018
Illustrations copyright © Claire Powell 2018

Visit our website at: www.harpercollins.co.uk
Printed in China

Princess Scallywag and the Brave, Brave Knight

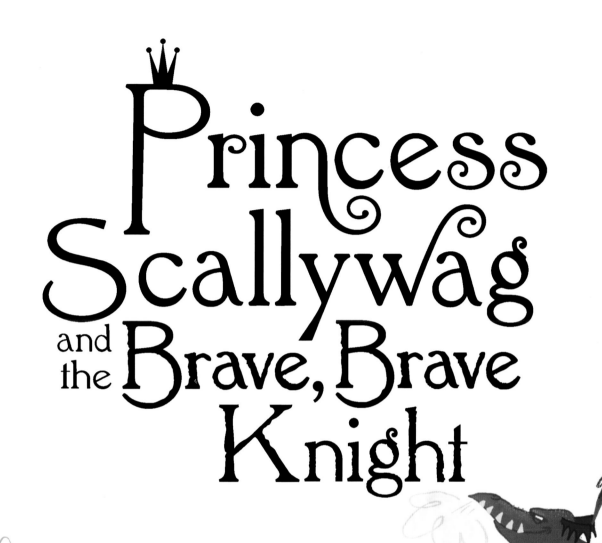

MARK SPERRING

illustrated by

CLAIRE POWELL

HarperCollins *Children's Books*

One morning,
the Queen looked out
of her window and saw
two things . . .

The first thing she saw
was the kingdom's bravest
knight skipping across
the drawbridge.

And the second thing
she saw was . . .

a BIG, BOTHERSOME... dragon!

"You down there!" called the Queen to the knight.

"If you rid this land of that **bothersome dragon**, you'll win the hand of my **delightful** daughter, Princess Scallywag."

"Me, marry the princess?!" spluttered the knight. "I couldn't **possibly** do that . . .

I've heard she takes baths in the moat with the **frogs** and the **toads!**"

The dragon ignored their foolish tittle-tattle and . . .

Raaaaaaaa!

. . . carried on as usual.

"Could you **stop** that endless 'Raaaa'-ing for just one moment?" hissed the Queen.

"But it's only fair you marry Princess Scallywag," she said. "If you save the kingdom, you marry the princess. It happens in all the stories all the time— don't you know?"

"I do know," said the knight, "but unfortunately, I've heard . . .

your daughter's feet smell like two slabs of **moldy old** cheese!"

"Mere rumor!" sniffed the Queen with a wave of her hanky, and she carried on with the marriage plans regardless.

"So . . . after you've done you-know-what to you-know-who . . .

we'll boil up his bones, pickle his scales, and roast his toes over a nice, warm fire. Then we'll serve him up on a bed of chopped tomatoes and green lettuce leaves which will be **perfect** for the wedding feast!"

The dragon felt his blood boil.
Smoke **billowed** from his nostrils...

But just as he was about to reduce
the Queen, her castle and her whole
bothersome kingdom to ash—the
knight stomped an armored foot...

"Seriously," said the knight, "I **really** couldn't **possibly** marry Princess Scallywag! You see . . .

I've heard she flies her grubby old undies from the top of the flagpole!"

"Surely you wouldn't let a pair of harmless panties stop you from marrying my daughter, would you?" scowled the Queen.

"Maybe . . ." said the knight.

"Well I'm not having **this** story end without Princess Scallywag getting married and living

Happily
Ever After!

So... **you'll** just have to marry her!" said the Queen, pointing **pointedly** at...

the **dragon!**

"Me?" gasped the dragon,
suddenly looking flustered.
"But I've only come here to burn
down the entire kingdom!"

"No excuses!" said the Queen.

"Princess Scallywag," she called,
"a lovely dragon actually
wants to marry you, so come
out now and show yourself,
before he changes
his mind and . . .

...flies off!"

"Oh dear," chuckled the Queen
once the dragon had gone.
"I don't think he liked the sound
of Princess Scallywag **at all!**"

"They **never** do!" laughed
Princess Scallywag,
throwing off her armor
with a triumphant

Clunk!

"But we always have
such **fun** getting
rid of them!"

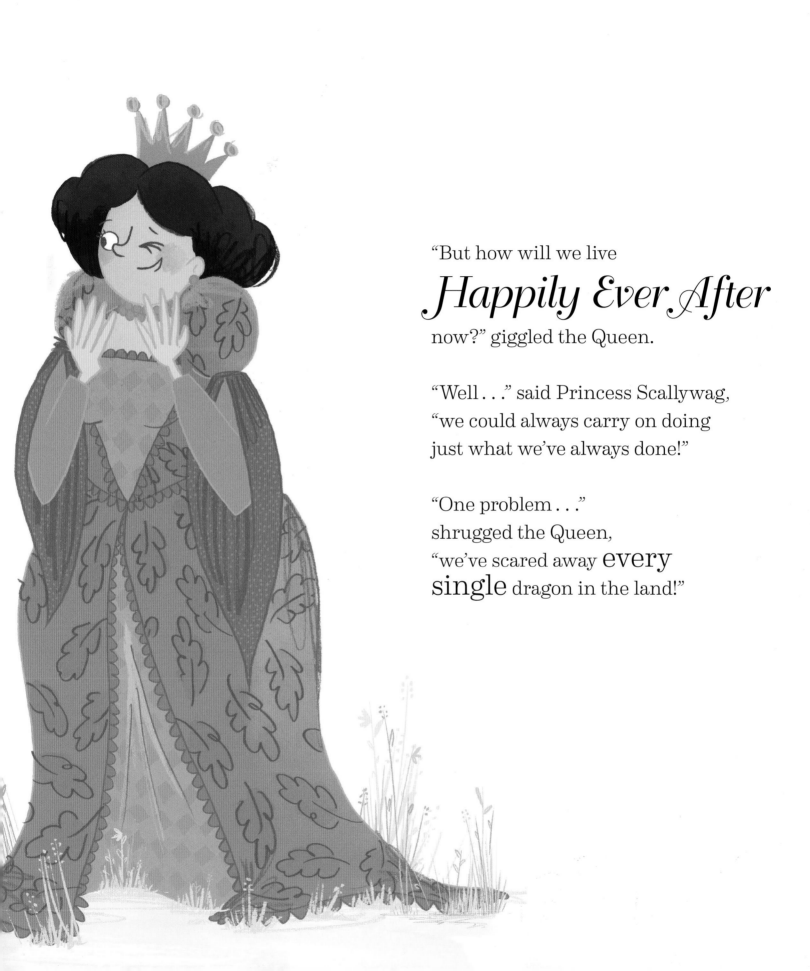

"But how will we live

Happily Ever After

now?" giggled the Queen.

"Well..." said Princess Scallywag,
"we could always carry on doing
just what we've always done!"

"One problem..."
shrugged the Queen,
"we've scared away every
single dragon in the land!"

"Then we'll just have to move on to **BIGGER** and **BETTER THINGS**…" grinned Princess Scallywag.

And later that afternoon…

THUMP!

SHUDDER!

Grrrr!

...that's
EXACTLY
what they did!